BEATRICE BLUE

Once Upon A UNICORN HORN

Frances Lincoln
First Editions

Once upon a magic forest,
there was a little girl called June.

June knew the woods were
full of treasures waiting
to be discovered.

She loved to climb
through the tallest trees
to find castles,

and peer through the bushes
to find magic wands.

Then one day June
found the greatest
treasure of all...

Tiny magic horses learning to fly!
June couldn't believe it.

They shook their
soft fur,

fluttered their sparkly tails,

and whizzed into the air.

But there was one little horse that wasn't flying.
He looked very sad.

"Are you ok little horsie?"
June asked. "Can't you fly?"
He shook his head.

"I can help you,"
said June. "We just have
to make your fur shake
and your tail flutter."

So they tried rolling,

and jumping,

and running really fast,

but nothing happened.

"I guess we'll have to use
magic," said June.

She rummaged through her box of treasures
until she found her most powerful magic wand.

June swooshed a big swoosh
and wished a big wish...

But it still didn't work.
The little horse was sadder than ever,

and so was June.

As soon as she got home, Mum and Dad could
tell something was wrong. Not even her
favourite dinner could make
her smile.

June told them all about the tiny horse.
"I tried to help but my magic wand didn't work,"
she said. "I think it's broken."

"Don't worry," Mum and Dad said.
"We can fix it together!"

"How do we fix my wand?" said June
"Let's start by trying to cheer up
your friend," said Mum.

"Tomorrow, we'll think of all
the things that a little horse
might like," said Dad.

The next morning,
everyone thought hard.
"Something sweet?"
said June.

"Something happy?"
said Dad.

"What about something
to share?" said Mum.

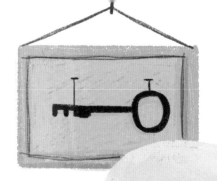

"I know," said June.
"Let's give him an
ice-cream!"

Just before she left, Mum and Dad
whispered a magic formula to make sure the
ice-cream tasted super sweet.

June couldn't wait
to cheer up her friend.
She ran as fast as she could,

but it was a little too fast.
She tripped, then the ice cream
slipped out of her hand, and...

It was a disaster.

But then June saw that the little horse liked his new horn very much.

After all, it was perfectly delicious!

He smiled,
    then he laughed,

then he shook his soft fur
and fluttered his sparkly tail...

and it worked!
It was the happiest day ever.
Ever since, magic horses
have been called unicorns,

for they all wear horns
to remember the day
when a little girl was
a good friend.

June often wears hers too and she never forgets the magic formula.

MY MAGIC IS DEEP INSIDE

DON'T NEED A WAND TO FLY

BETTWS

To Mum and Dad,
who showed me where to find magic.

Big thanks and love to Dani, Ali, Zoë and Katie
for the huge help and encouragement.

Brimming with creative inspiration, how-to projects, and useful information to enrich your everyday life, Quarto Knows is a favourite destination for those pursuing their interests and passions. Visit our site and dig deeper with our books into your area of interest: Quarto Creates, Quarto Cooks, Quarto Homes, Quarto Lives, Quarto Drives, Quarto Explores, Quarto Gifts, or Quarto Kids.

Text and illustrations © 2019 Beatrice Blue

First published in 2019 by First Editions under Frances Lincoln Children's Books,
an imprint of The Quarto Group.
The Old Brewery, 6 Blundell Street, London N7 9BH, United Kingdom.
T (0)20 7700 6700 F (0)20 7700 8066 www.QuartoKnows.com

The right of Beatrice Blue to be identified as the author and illustrator and of this work has been asserted by her in accordance with the Copyright, Designs and Patents Act, 1988 (United Kingdom).

A catalogue record for this book is available from the British Library.

ISBN 978-1-78603-588-2

The illustrations were created digitally
Set in Lelo

Published by Rachel Williams
Designed by Zoë Tucker
Edited by Katie Cotton
Production by Kate O'Riordan and Jenny Cundill

Manufactured in Shenzhen, China HH112018

FSC
MIX
Paper from
responsible sources
FSC® C017606
www.fsc.org